THIS CANDLEWICK BOOK BELONGS TO:

_____

_____

_____

_____

For David, Megan, and Mary

First U.S. paperback edition 1997

The Library of Congress has cataloged the hardcover edition as follows:

Prater, John.
The greatest show on earth / John Prater.—1st U.S. ed.
Summary: Young Harry feels useless because he lacks the talents
that other family members have as circus performers.
ISBN 1-56402-563-2 (hardcover)
[1. Circus—Fiction. 2. Self-esteem—Fiction.] I. Title.
PZ7.P8867Gr   1995
[E]—dc20   94-24991

ISBN 0-7636-0105-5 (paperback)

2 4 6 8 10 9 7 5 3 1

Printed in Hong Kong

This book was typeset in Century Old Style.
The pictures were done in pencil and watercolor.

Candlewick Press
2067 Massachusetts Avenue
Cambridge, Massachusetts 02140

Ringling Bros. and Barnum & Bailey

THE GREATEST SHOW

— ON EARTH —

JOHN PRATER

CANDLEWICK PRESS

CAMBRIDGE, MASSACHUSETTS

Ladies and gentlemen, boys and girls, welcome to Ringling Bros.!
It's The Greatest Show On Earth.
There's magic and daring, amazing acts and incredible tricks . . .

and there's Harry. That's me!

This is Mom and Dad, who fly on the high trapeze.

And this is me . . . Oops!

This is my brilliant sister Sue. She can juggle almost anything.

And this is me . . . Ouch!

This is Wobble and Wilt—the cleverest acrobats you've ever seen.

And this is me . . . Whoops!

Abracadabra! This is Mr. Mysterio, conjuring flowers and fireworks from his hat.

And this is me . . . Bang!

This is Grandad on his wild whizzing wheels.

And this is me . . . Oooer! Yikes!

This is Grandma, who's so strong she can lift a trailer with one hand.

And this is me . . . Oh, dear!

And this is Wellington the dog. He tops the bill with his amazing balancing act. I can't fly through the air or juggle or balance or do magic tricks, so I take care of Wellington.

This is me.

Tonight's the night of the big show.
Ladies and gentlemen, boys and girls, silence, please,
for Wellington's amazing balancing act!

But Wellington has seen a mouse and . . . *WOOF! SQUEAK!* Oh, no!

CLATTER! WHOOSH! Help!

BOING! WHEE! I'm flying!

SWOOSH! SWING! This is fun!

WOBBLE! WHIZZ! I can do it! Hooray!

Hooray for Mom and Dad the fliers, my sister Sue the juggler, Wobble and Wilt the acrobats, Mr. Mysterio the magician, Grandad the unicyclist, Grandma the strongwoman, my dog Wellington who walks the wire . . . and who else?

Let's hear it now! As loud as you can!
HOORAY FOR HARRY THE CLOWN!
That's me!

JOHN PRATER wrote this story because he wanted "to portray someone who was not very good at anything. In Harry's case the problem is confounded because everyone else in his family is amazingly good at something. Yet he does what everyone must do eventually: he finds his niche." John Prater also wrote and illustrated *"No!" said Joe,* as well as conceiving and illustrating *Once Upon a Time* and *Once Upon a Picnic,* both written by Vivian French.